OVER PROTECTION ON TENNAGERS

ITS ABOUT WHAT A TENNAGER HAD TO SUFFER , TEENAGER THOUGHTS THEIR FEELING

CHAHAT VISHWAKARMA

Made with ♥ on the Notion Press Platform
www.notionpress.com

TEENAGERS

WHAT IS TEENAGER ?

THIS QUESTION COMES IN EVERYBODY MIND

NOW FIRST LET US TALK ABOUT WHAT IS TEENAGER ?

- The life of a teenager seems to change daily. Constantly exposed to new ideas, social situations and people, teenagers work to develop their personalities and interests during this time of great change. Before their teenage years, these adolescents focused on school, play, and gaining approval from their parents.

- A teenager, or teen, is someone who is between 13 and 19 years old. They are called teenagers because the number of their age contains the suffix "teen". The word "teenager" is often associated with adolescence. Most neurologists consider the brain still developing into a person's early or mid-20s. A person becomes a teenager when they become 13 years old. It ends when they become 20 years old. Teenagers who are between 13 and 17 years old are considered both children and teenagers in most countries. Teenagers who are 18 and 19 years old may be regarded as both teenagers and adults.

The way the word is used varies. Most societies have rites of passage to mark the change from childhood to adulthood. These ceremonies may be quite elaborate.[1] During puberty, rapid mental and physical development occurs. Adolescence is the name for this transition period from childhood to adulthood.[source?]

"Teenager" is mainly an English word, as many foreign languages do not include a suffix in their translations of the numbers 13 to 19. In non-English speaking countries, people between these ages may be called adolescents, youths, young adults, or just children, depending on the culture.

- The life of a teenager seems to change daily. Constantly exposed to new ideas, social situations and people, teenagers work to develop their personalities and interests during this time of great change. Before their teenage years, these adolescents focused on school, play, and gaining approval from their parents.

Contents

Foreword

ABOUT THIS BOOK

TEENAGERS DEPRESSIONDepressionFeeling sad is a healthy, normal part of life. For some people sadness comes out of nowhere, triggered by something as simple as a song that comes on the radio. It ebbs and flows. But for others, feelings of sadness won't go away and the origin of the sadness is hard to discern. It is not something they can "snap out of" or control. It causes feelings and thoughts that won't go away. Many lose interest in normal daily activities, lack energy, and have trouble concentrating. These are all signs of depression, a mood disorder also referred to as clinical depression or major depressive disorder.

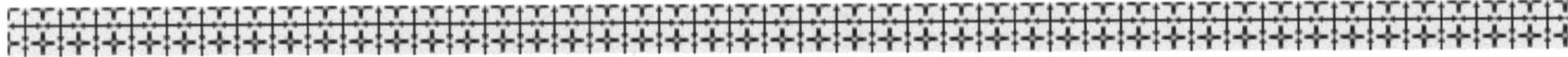

Preface

TEENAGERS FEELINGS

TEENAGER FEELINGS

- when you are a teenager you have that the pressure to fit it and also having an identity crisis. Teenagers are going through a roller coaster of emotions you feel self consistence or depressed. teens have a lot of stress and pressure to deal with social life,school work,and home life it can be overwhelming.
- A teen may have a higher risk for depression if he or she has a family history of it. Trauma, stress, and abuse can

also make a teen prone to it. Symptoms include feelings of sadness, despair, and guilt. A teen may lose interest in activities and have problems sleeping and eating.

- Adolescence is the transition between childhood to adulthood. It involves a lot of physical, psychological, and behavioural changes. Adolescence years start with puberty. In girls, it starts at the age of 12 or 13, whereas in boys it varies from 13-15 years. Physical changes are very prominent in these years.

Acknowledgements

I GOT INSPIRATION OF WRITING THIS BOOK FROM

Thakur Rudra Pratap Singh

Thakur Rudra Pratap Singh

- Thakur Rudra Pratap Singh (born on June 3, 2009) of Najibabad, Uttar Pradesh, is appreciated for writing a book titled 'Fiction Novels' (ISBN No. 979-88-85556-05-7), published by Notion Press. The book, which consists of motivational stories to help people come out of depression, was published on January 8, 2022, as confirmed on February 17, 2022.

- THANK YOU **Thakur Rudra Pratap Singh** FOR WRITINGBEAUTIFUL BOOKS AND GIVING ME INSPIRATION.

Teenagers

STUDY PRESSURE ON TEENAGERS

- Three to nine per cent of teenagers meet the criteria for depression at any one time, and at the end of adolescence, as many as 20% of teenagers report a lifetime prevalence of depression. Usual care by primary care physicians fails to recognize 30-50% of depressed patients.
-
- The study highlights the common but ignored problem of depression in adolescence. We recommend that teachers and parents be made aware of this problem with the help of school counselors so that the depressed adolescent can be identified and helped rather than suffer silently.
- Adolescent depression may affect the teen's socialization, family relations, and performance at school, often

with potentially serious long-term consequences. Adolescents with depression are at risk for increased hospitalizations, recurrent depressions, psychosocial impairment, alcohol abuse, and antisocial behaviors as they grow up.

CHAPTER ONE

A SHORT STORY ABOUT A TEENAGER

There was girl name Minji. She was 14 years old she was a Teenager girl . She realizes many things after becoming a Teenager . she think when she was a kid these things never happen with her . she had never suffer from these problems like she get scolded by her parents , her parents force her , they never allow her to go out from home for long time . because her parents were very over protective .

STRICT PARENTS

these things happen with her in this age but never happen in a age of a kid. she was very depressed ater bearing these things. she think that her friend was very lucky because her parents were not that much of over protective but

her friend hanni thinks that her parents are very careless the don't love her they don't take care of her . they never say anything to her

and yes it was true that mostly some parents become very over protective and some not .

parents should not become that much of over protective or that much of careless

TRUE

they should let their child do whatever their child want but never force them to do that thing that they don't like .let them take their own diccisions because they are not a kid now .parents have to understood their child that he or she can take his or her own diccisions.

but also parents should not become that much of careless let them do whatever they want but if they are moving on wrong side than you should stop them by doing this and one most important message for all parents never compare your child with others because every child has different talent .maybe your child have unique talent .

WRITTEN BY

Chahat Vishwakarma

TEENAGERS

- Teenagers are passing through that phase of their life when they neither qualify as adults nor as children.

  I am a teenager. I am a challenge but I am worth it. With depression, elation pimples, funky hair styles, attitude, no fear, shyness, ambition, mischievous, different in a group, confident yet insecure ... a walking contradiction. I am at the pinnacle of age non-conformance, while trying very hard to socially conform, a rebel, looking for a cause.

  The world looks unfair, the rules twisted... a conspiracy I cry out – “they are not letting me grow and develop and be myself”. “They”, an all encompassing ‘Anyone who dares to tell me.

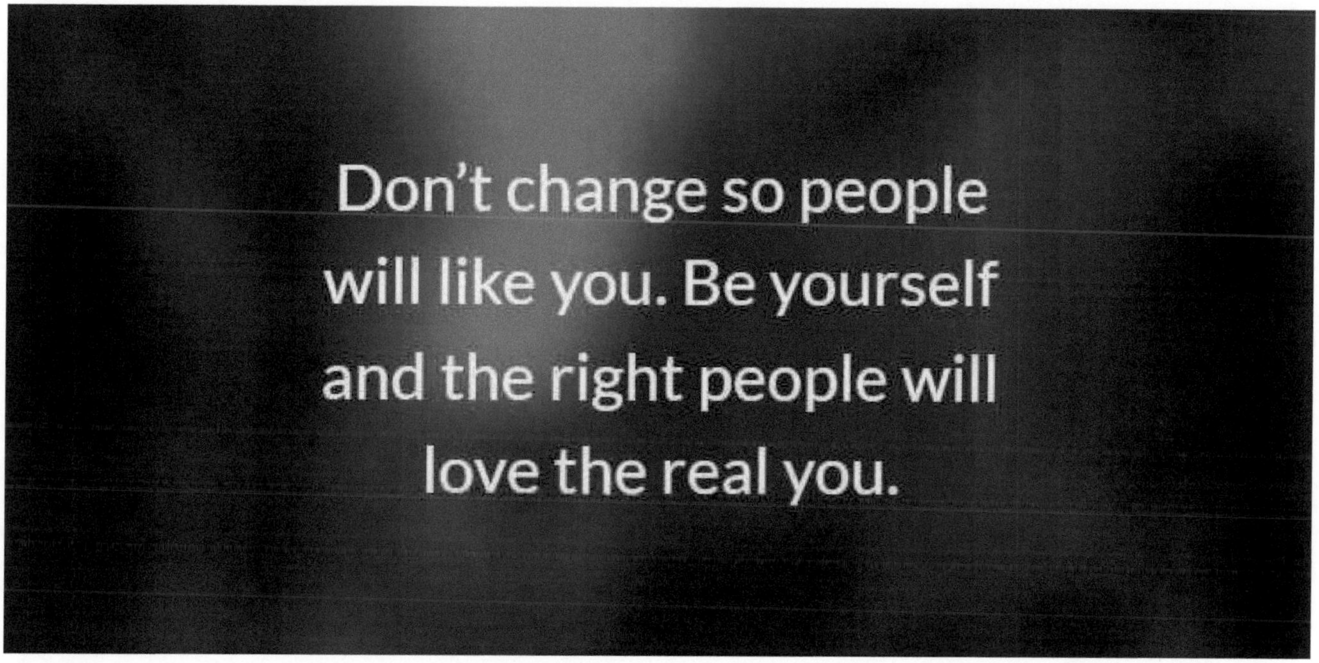

Don’t change so people
will like you. Be yourself
and the right people will
love the real you.

JUST SPEAK YOURSELF

Printed by Libri Plureos GmbH in Hamburg,
Germany